KT-365-414

DC
COMICS™

BATMAN™

TALES OF THE
BATCAVE

THE CLOWN PRINCE
OF CARDS

by
MICHAEL DAHL

illustrated by
LUCIANO VECCHIO

Batman created by
BOB KANE WITH BILL FINGER

raintree

04394697

Raintree is an imprint of Capstone Global Library Limited, a
company incorporated in England and Wales having its registered
office at 264 Banbury Road, Oxford, OX2 7DY – Registered company
number: 6695582

www.raintree.co.uk
myorders@raintree.co.uk

Text © Capstone Global Library Limited 2017
The moral rights of the proprietor have been asserted.
Copyright © 2017 DC Comics.
BATMAN and all related characters and elements are trademarks of and © DC Comics.
(s16).

STAR37779

All rights reserved. No part of this publication may be reproduced in any form or by any means
(including photocopying or storing it in any medium by electronic means and whether or not
transiently or incidentally to some other use of this publication) without the written permission
of the copyright owner, except in accordance with the provisions of the Copyright, Designs and
Patents Act 1988 or under the terms of a licence issued by the Copyright Licensing Agency,
Saffron House, 6–10 Kirby Street, London EC1N 8TS (www.cla.co.uk). Applications for the
copyright owner's written permission should be addressed to the publisher.

ISBN 978 1 4747 2911 6
20 19 18 17 16
10 9 8 7 6 5 4 3 2 1

British Library Cataloguing in Publication Data
A full catalogue record for this book is available from the British Library.

Every effort has been made to contact copyright holders of material reproduced in this book.
Any omissions will be rectified in subsequent printings if notice is given to the publisher.

All the internet addresses (URLs) given in this book were valid at the time of going to press.
However, due to the dynamic nature of the internet, some addresses may have changed, or
sites may have changed or ceased to exist since publication. While the author and publisher
regret any inconvenience this may cause readers, no responsibility for any such changes can
be accepted by either the author or the publisher.

Editor: Christopher Harbo
Designer: Bob Lentz
Production Specialist: Kathy McColley

Printed and bound in China.

CONTENTS

This is the BATCAVE.

GIANT
JOKER
PLAYING
CARD

It is the secret headquarters of Batman and his crime-fighting partner, Robin.

Hundreds of trophies, awards and souvenirs fill the Batcave's hidden rooms. Each one tells a story of danger, villainy and victory.

This is the tale of a giant Joker playing card! And why this trophy now stands in the Batcave . . .

CHAPTER 1

THE KING'S TREASURE

Two dark figures stand on top of Gotham City's tallest skyscraper.

They swoop through the darkness on long ropes, and swing through a tall open window.

"Batman! Robin!" shouts a man, as they drop inside a luxury hotel room.

"Evening, Commissioner Gordon," says Batman. "Any clues to the missing treasure?"

"Not yet," Gordon says. "But thanks for sending Ace to help us out."

A large dog sniffs the rugs and furniture. It is Ace, the Bat-Hound. He is working undercover without his mask and cape.

"How could a thief steal the national treasure of Prankistan from this penthouse suite?" says Gordon.

"And from the tallest building in the city!"
says the Boy Wonder. "It's a puzzle."

"Did you post guards in the lifts?"
Batman asks.

"Yes," says Gordon. "I even put security guards on the roof. No one has been seen up there except you tonight."

"This looks like an impossible crime!" Robin says, punching his glove.

CHAPTER 2

THE RULER'S EXIT

Another man bursts into the room. He wears a gold suit and a turban covered in jewels.

"Dynamic Duo!" he cries. "You are finding the treasure, no?"

"Don't worry, your Highness," says Gordon. "No one can hide from Batman and Robin."

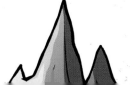

"You must help me," begs the King of Prankistan. "The royal cobra has been in my family for years."

"A snake is the national treasure?" whispers Robin to Batman.

"The emperor cobra of Prankistan is
the rarest snake in the world," Batman
whispers back.

The Bat-Hound barks from another room.

The crime-fighters and Commissioner Gordon quickly follow the dog's signal.

"What have you found, Ace?" says Robin.

The Bat-Hound has his paws on an open windowsill.

"The thief must have escaped through this window," says Batman.

"But how?" says Gordon. "We're on the top floor!"

YAAAAAAAAA!

A scream comes from the King of Prankistan in the other room.

Robin and Ace race back.

They find an empty room. A jewelled turban lies on the floor.

"The King has vanished!" cries the Boy Wonder.

Ace sniffs at the turban. Batman rushes to the open window and peers into the darkness.

Suddenly, a loud alarm blares from several streets away.

"Another robbery!" cries Batman.

CHAPTER 3

THE QUEEN'S CROWN

The Batmobile roars through the city streets, tracking the wail of the alarm.

The car screeches to a stop as two security guards hail the heroes.

"Look!" says one of the guards. He points towards the top of a nearby building.

QUEEN

MUSIC HALL

19

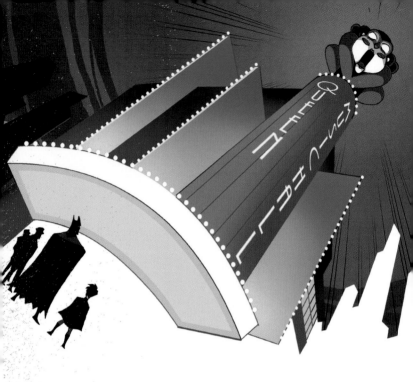

"The crown on the Queen Music Hall statue has vanished!" Robin cries.

"Another royal treasure gone!" says Batman.

"And another high-level robbery," says Robin.

"High is right," says one of the guards. "That sign is 30 metres above the ground."

"Is there a way up?" asks Batman.

"Only a metal spiral staircase," answers the guard. "And I was guarding the locked gate in front of it."

Suddenly, Ace the Bat-Hound begins to growl.

"Listen," says a guard. "Do you hear that humming sound?"

A sudden shadow passes swiftly above their heads.

A moment later another alarm shrieks several streets away.

"I sense a crime wave in the air," says Batman.

The Dynamic Duo and Ace rush back to
the Batmobile.

The vehicle roars into life and rockets
towards the new alarm.

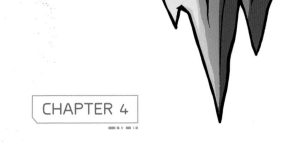

CHAPTER 4

THE JOKER'S WILD

"There it is, Batman!" cries Robin, pointing. "By the Regal department store's tenth floor!"

A flickering shape hovers high in the air near a broken window.

"Don't tell me that's a flying carpet!" says Robin.

"And it's next to the jewellery showroom!" says Batman.

A figure steps out of the broken window and on to the floating rectangle.

The shape glides down towards the Batmobile.

A weird laugh echoes through the night.

HAHAHAHAHA!

"The Joker!" shouts Robin.

"People have been calling me a card for years!" he shrieks. "So I finally made one of my own!"

The Joker stands on a giant playing card. A Joker!

"I've become quite the flying ace," he laughs.

The villain swoops towards the Dynamic
Duo. Batman and Robin leap out of the way.

Ace jumps out of the Batmobile and dashes
down a side street.

"I'm good at *attracting* attention," chuckles the Joker, rising above the heroes again. "But I hope I don't *repulse* you."

"Attract. Repulse," says the Dark Knight. "The Joker's flying card must be powered by an electromagnet."

"Its humming engine pushes and pulls him between any buildings made of metal," adds the Boy Wonder.

Batman and Robin pull Batarangs from their belts. They aim for the Clown Prince of Crime.

"Careful, Dynamic Duo!" warns the villain. "If you pull me down, you'll break my crown!"

The Joker flies low. The heroes glimpse a figure in a gold suit lying next to the villain.

"The King of Prankistan!" shouts Robin.

"Don't throw, Robin," orders Batman.
"We can't put the King's life in danger."

CHAPTER 5

THE UPPER HAND

The Joker stands high above Batman and Robin. His flying card hovers near the Regal building.

"Holding the King gives me the upper hand!" crows the criminal.

"Now I'm off to my next–"

A shadow appears at one of the building's windows. It growls and leaps at the Joker.

The villain is carried over the edge of his card and on to a nearby fire escape.

"It's Ace!" says Robin. "Good boy!"

With the Joker caught by Ace, the card floats harmlessly to the ground.

"The King is safe," says Batman with a smile. "Thanks to Ace, we'll recover the missing crown and the royal cobra."

"That crooked clown," says Robin. "He should have known an Ace always beats a Joker!"

EPILOGUE . . .

"Batman, can we keep the Joker's flying card in the Batcave?"

"As a reminder of how we dealt with that villain?"

"Yeah, it would be a shame to discard it."

"Suits me, Boy Wonder. How about you, Ace?"

"Woof! Woof!"

GLOSSARY

attract pull something towards something else

card clownishly amusing person; also a stiff, rectangular piece of paper used in games

commissioner person who is in charge of a government department

electromagnet temporary magnet created by an electric current

emperor leader of a country or group of countries

hover remain in one place in the air

penthouse flat or hotel room located on the top floor of a tall building

repulse drive or force back

security guards who watch over or protect something

turban head covering made by winding a long scarf around the head or around a cap

Discuss

1. Robin says the Joker's flying card uses magnetic power to push and pull him through the air. Do you know what he means?

2. The Joker likes to follow a theme when he commits his crimes. Based on the names of what he stole and where he went, can you work out his theme this time?

3. The Dynamic Duo and Ace work together as a team. Do you think Batman and Robin could have captured the Joker without Ace's help?

Write

1. The Joker uses his new invention, the flying card, to move around Gotham City. What would you do with a flying device like that? Write a paragraph about it.

2. The King of Prankistan's royal pet is a cobra. If you could have an unusual pet, what would you choose? Describe it and write how you would take care of it.

3. The heroes in this story are sometimes called by other names: the Dynamic Duo, the Dark Knight, and the Boy Wonder. If you were a super hero, what would your powers be? And what nicknames would you have?

AUTHOR

Michael Dahl is the prolific author of the best-selling *Goodnight Baseball* picture book and more than 200 other books for children and young adults. In the United States, he has won the AEP Distinguished Achievement Award three times for his non-fiction, a Teachers' Choice Award from *Learning* magazine, and a Seal of Excellence from the Creative Child Awards. He is also the author of the Hocus Pocus Hotel mystery series and the Dragonblood books. Dahl currently lives in Minneapolis, Minnesota, USA.

ILLUSTRATOR

Luciano Vecchio was born in 1982 and is based in Buenos Aires, Argentina. Freelance artist for many projects at Marvel and DC Comics, his work has been seen in print and online around the world. He has illustrated many DC Super Heroes books for Capstone, and some of his recent comic work includes *Beware the Batman*, *Green Lantern: The Animated Series*, *Young Justice*, *Ultimate Spider-Man*, and his creator-owned web-comic, *Sereno*.